The Sugar Chair Stories

Volume One

Mark and Alexandra Milliron

Balboa Press books may be ordered through booksellers or by contacting:

Balboa Press
A Division of Hay House
1663 Liberty Drive
Bloomington, IN 47403
www.balboapress.com
1 (877) 407-4847

ISBN: 978-1-9822-5295-3 (sc)
ISBN: 978-1-9822-5294-6 (e)

Library of Congress Control Number: 2020915097

Print information available on the last page.

Balboa Press rev. date: 08/26/2020

BALBOA.PRESS
A DIVISION OF HAY HOUSE

Volume One

The three stories that follow mean to speak to the head and heart. They are the first in a series of stories we will produce in the coming years. As you read, keep in mind that the "sugar chair" is not a thing; it is a way. It's a way of helping ourselves and our children slow this crazy world down, see clearer through our own eyes and the eyes of others, and own and act on our strategies for "sweetening things up." Each story focuses on a certain audience: Littles (3-8 years old), Middles (8-12 years old), and Olders (12 years old and up). Our thinking is that Olders should read all three, Middles the first two, and Littles the first one. But in the end, you decide what's right for you and your crew. We hope you enjoy!

Mark & Alexandra Milliron

Table of Contents

The Sugar Chair: Beginnings 1

The Sugar Chair: Moving In 15

The Sugar Chair: Coming Home 27

About the Authors:.. 39

Story 1 – For Littles (3-8yrs old)
The Sugar Chair: Beginnings

Being a puppy is hard work. At least that's what Buddy thought. He only joined the family a month ago, so he was still learning who everyone is, where everything is, and how the whole food thing works.

From what Buddy could tell, Mom and Dad were in charge. James and Taylor were much smaller—and more fun. James really liked music. He played the piano all the time. But sometimes he didn't seem very happy about it. He also liked trains. He spent hours playing with train cars, setting up tracks on his train table, and talking about different kinds of trains with Dad. Just yesterday, Buddy learned that chewing train cars was not a good thing.

Of everyone in the family, Taylor spent the most time with Buddy. She liked to run and play with him a lot—outside and inside. Also, she was the best hugger and tummy rubber. And even though she was the smallest person in the family, she seemed to have the biggest smile. Most of all, Buddy really liked Taylor because he thought she was still figuring things out, just like he was.

One of the hardest things about being a puppy for Buddy was staying out of trouble. He didn't always know what's OK to chew, who's OK to rough house with, and where it's OK to go to the bathroom. That last one seemed pretty important to Mom and Dad. They usually told him not to worry when he was in trouble though. He was still learning.

Being the little one seemed hard for Taylor too. She got in trouble almost as much as Buddy. She didn't always know what's OK to throw, when it's OK to be loud—especially if Mom or Dad were on the phone—and what's OK to take apart. That last one seemed pretty important to Mom and Dad. They usually told her not to worry when she made a mistake though, because she was still learning.

But once in a while, when the trouble seemed big, they would take Taylor to the Sugar Chair.

Slow Down
Look Around
Figure Out How to Sweeten Things Up

5

The Sugar Chair was a gift from Grandma. Buddy liked Grandma. She and Grandpa lived nearby and came over to visit a lot. She was especially good at sneaking him treats. He heard that she had been a schoolteacher for 40 years. That seemed like a long time. Grandma said she used the Sugar Chair in her classes to help her kids figure things out.

Grandpa smiled when he talked about the Sugar Chair. He said, "That chair got a lot of use. Your Grandma wanted her kids to learn how to 'train their brain', not just sit and stew." Grandpa said when her students got older, they would come back and talk about how they built their own big-person sugar chair, or how they were using one with their own kids.

All Buddy knew was that Grandma was sweet to him and always told him to give her "some sugar" when she came over. So, he thought it made sense that the Sugar Chair came from her.

The Sugar Chair was a white rocking chair that had a little plaque on the back that read:

Slow Down,
Look Around,
Figure Out How to Sweeten Things Up

Buddy liked that. And it seemed to work for Taylor too.

One time, Taylor and Buddy were playing fetch in the house. Buddy was banging into walls and bouncing off couches as he chased after the bright-yellow ball. It was so fun. But then Taylor threw the ball under James's train table. Buddy ran fast after the ball, but he had a hard time stopping on the super slippery floor. He ended up sliding right into the leg of the table.

After Buddy smashed into the leg, the whole table tipped over. Train tracks and cars came crashing down on his head. He and Taylor looked at each other. They knew this was not good.

9

The crash was loud. James was louder. He was so upset. The train track that he worked on all week was destroyed, and a couple of his cars were broken. Mom and Dad came running in. James was yelling at Taylor. Taylor was yelling at James. Buddy was hiding from them all. Taylor kept saying, "It was an accident! It was an accident!" That didn't seem to help. Before long, she was crying. James was crying. Buddy was crying. It was a mess.

Buddy watched as Mom walked Taylor out of the playroom and over to the Sugar Chair. He could see how upset Taylor was. As Mom sat her down, she told her, "Taylor, I want you to take a few minutes here. You know what to do. Slow down, look around, and figure out how to sweeten things up. When I come back, we can talk some more."

Taylor had learned how the Sugar Chair worked. She was supposed to "slow the world down for a minute," Grandma would say. Take a breath. Take another. Try to get to a calmer place before doing anything else.

Slow Down
Look Around
Figure Out How to Sweeten Things Up

Then she's supposed to look around, see things through her eyes, but also try to see things the way other people might. How does James see the crash? How does Mom? How does Dad? How are they feeling? What are they thinking? Why?

Grandma would say that after slowing down and looking around, you're in a much better place to figure out how to sweeten things up. The trouble happened. There's no changing that. But what can you do about it now or later to make things better?

It took Mom and Dad a while to calm James down and clean up the mess. By then, Taylor was ready. When Mom came back, she got down on one knee, looked Taylor in the eyes, and asked calmly, "What do you think?"

Taylor said, "I shouldn't have been playing fetch with Buddy in the house. It's probably better to do that outside next time."

Mom gave her a hug. "What else?"

"I need to say sorry to James. I feel bad that we broke his train. And I probably need to ask him if he wants me to help pick things up." Taylor added.

Mom said, "that sounds like a good plan." She took Taylor's hand and they walked out to talk with James.

Buddy thought it was a good plan too.

Story 2 – For Middles (8-12)
The Sugar Chair:
Moving In

15

Moving is hard work. At least that's what Buddy thought. The family moved into the new, big, white house a few weeks ago. After five years in the old house, it was hard for Buddy to figure out who these neighbors were, how this crazy "doggy door" was supposed to work, and where the snacks were.

Taylor was having an even harder time. They lost some of her favorite stuff in the move: her basketball, two of her posters, and even some of her clothes. She wasn't sure about the new room either. It was bigger, but it made her feel smaller. It didn't feel like her place, and the house definitely didn't either.

Most of all, Taylor was having a hard time leaving her friends. She left so many buddies behind in the old neighborhood. Now she was supposed to make "new friends." Everyone—Mom, Dad, Grandma, Grandpa—kept saying that. But she was too busy missing her old friends right now.

Making "new friends" didn't make any sense to Taylor anyway. Christina and Jayla were her best friends in the world. They had so many memories together. It was so easy to find things to do with them, and so fun. How would she ever find that again. Lying in bed at night was the worst time, because all she thought about was how easy and exciting things used to be.

It didn't seem to be as hard for James. He jumped right into band practice and started hanging out with boys who lived down the street. His room seemed to be set up in no time. And he was already having other kids over. Buddy thought some of these new kids were scary. He even barked and growled at a couple of them. But James told him not to worry, "these guys are my friends, Buddy!" Taylor couldn't believe he was calling them *friends* after only a few days.

On the second day of school, Taylor walked home from the bus stop in tears. Buddy saw her sneak through the front door and run up to her room.

Buddy could tell she didn't want to talk about it with anyone. She didn't want anyone to tell her that "it's going to be OK," or that "it's going to get better." She just wanted to be sad . . . and be alone. But Buddy knew that he was different. She needed him to come up quickly. Taylor liked to hug him and cuddle close, especially when she was sad. Probably because he didn't try to say anything.

After almost an hour of crying, Buddy decided he had to do something. He thought about what had helped in the past when trouble popped up. That's when he jumped off the bed, walked over to the corner of the room, and yanked at the comforter and the clothes stacked up in the corner. Taylor thought maybe Buddy hid some food under there or something. But then she saw what was underneath. The Sugar Chair.

"Buddy, I didn't do anything wrong. Why are you bringing out the Sugar Chair," Taylor asked? Then she remembered what Grandma says: The Sugar Chair isn't about being in trouble. It's about learning how to sweeten things up.

The more she thought about it, Taylor realized that things needed some serious sweetening. She looked at the plaque on the chair again. In her mind, she could hear her Grandma saying the words. And her Mom too.

Slow Down,
Look Around,
Figure Out How to Sweeten Things Up

Then Taylor sat down and took a deep breath. She was trying to do what grandma always says to, "slow the world's spinning down—at least for a few minutes." After a while, she took some time to think about how she saw the move. Then she thought about how hard the move was on Mom, Dad, James, and even Buddy. She also thought about how the new kids were seeing her. Over the last two days, teachers and kids tried to talk to her, but she was so sad and mad, she sometimes didn't even respond. "I probably don't look like good friend material," she thought to herself.

After calming down and trying to see things differently, Taylor began to plan for the sweetening. If she wanted this new place to work, she'd have to *do some work*. Setting up her room would help. Then she'd be excited to have friends over.

She also realized that she'd have to gather the courage to meet new people. She was smart enough to know that just like the old neighborhood, some kids would be nice, some would be mean, and some would be in between. She'd search out the nice ones, and start *being* a nice one. Maybe there were other new kids who were having a hard time too. Maybe she could help them. Of course, she'd still be sad from time to time and would miss the old house. But this new plan seemed to be much sweeter in the long run.

"Buddy, you're the best, if you didn't already know it," she said, as she gave him a big bear hug and wrestled with him on the floor.

"You know what, Buddy. I'm going to try to make this moving thing work. But first, I'm going to go downstairs and get some food—and maybe even a snack for you!"

"That sounds like a really good plan," Buddy thought.

The Sugar Chair: Coming Home

27

Being in a family is hard work. At least that's what Buddy thought. People are always coming and going, and they seem to be getting older faster. In the last ten years, it got harder for Buddy to know where the kids where, how often they'd come home from work or college, and whether they'd bring him some good treats!

Today, James and Taylor were supposed to be coming home for a big family dinner. James was first to arrive. He had a wife and a baby now, which confused Buddy a little. How could James, who was still a kid in Buddy's eyes, have a baby? But he thought the wife was nice—she always gave him a snuggly hug when she came over. The baby didn't say much. But it was a cute little thing. Buddy would just stare at the baby sometimes, waiting for it to do something that would explain all the attention everyone gave it.

Mom was so happy to have James and crew home. But she still seemed sad. She had a big smile when she hugged them as they came in the front door, but Buddy could see, she wasn't smiling on the inside. He thought it probably had to do with the trouble Grandma was having.

A few years ago, Grandma and Grandpa moved in with Mom, Dad, and Buddy. Buddy loved Grandma and Grandpa, so he was excited about the move. Grandpa wasn't a big eater. That meant when Mom put too much food on his plate, Buddy got the leftovers. Grandpa would throw him the bites and Buddy would catch them in the air. It was a good partnership. Grandma liked to play with plants in the garden, and she talked to Buddy the whole time she was outside. Even better, whenever she worked outside, she snuck him sweet treats.

Buddy liked Grandpa and Grandma moving in, a lot.

It got harder after a few months though. Grandma began forgetting things. Then she started forgetting more things. Sometimes she would stand and touch her old stand-up piano and just look lost, and other times she would seem frightened. One time she went for a walk and no one could find her. Through it all, everyone tried their best to help Grandma. However, she seemed to get a little tired of all the fuss.

Then, a few months ago, she had to move to a special place so she would be safe, and so doctors could care for her. It was hard on Grandpa. It was especially hard on Mom. She wanted Grandma to stay home. But the doctors said it was best that she stayed where "special" nurses and doctors could take care of her.

Taylor was away at college now. But she came home often. Buddy was never happier than when Taylor's car rolled into the driveway. He couldn't jump like he used to. But Taylor walking in the house sure made him try! This time, though, she had been away for almost 3 months. That was much too long, Buddy thought. He may need to get her in the Sugar Chair over that!

When Taylor came in, she could tell Buddy needed extra love. He pushed in front of everyone. No one was going to get in on the hugs before him. After Buddy, Mom was next in line. Taylor hugged Mom longer than usual. She could tell that Mom needed extra love too.

After a big dinner, Mom and Taylor told everyone to go in the living room so they could take over the kitchen and "clean up and catch up." They looked forward to their clean-up and catch-up thing, especially if Taylor was away for a while. Buddy learned early on that staying behind in the kitchen during these times meant he would get lots of extra snacks.

Mom and Taylor talked for a long time. This wasn't the loud talking and louder laughing that usually happens when these two clean. Mom was worried about James and his new wife, and the baby. She was also worried about Dad and some things going on at her work. Still, when Mom was talking about Grandma moving to the special place, you could tell she was having a hard time. Of course, Mom was worried about Grandpa not having Grandma with him. But there was something else, something more.

Grandma was forgetting more. She was forgetting her own name, where she was, and what day it was. But today had been especially hard, Mom said. When she went to visit her at the special place, Grandma didn't know who Mom was, she couldn't recognize her. She thought she was one of the volunteers who would come to their rooms. Mom started crying hard now. Taylor didn't know what to say. She just reached out and hugged Mom even harder and even longer this time.

After a few minutes, Taylor took Mom's hand and walked her out to the backyard. Buddy didn't get out the door in time to join in, so he was looking out the window at them. Taylor and Mom went out on the back porch and sat in two comfy chairs looking out at the soft pink sunset and shady green trees. He couldn't hear what they were saying. But after a few minutes, he figured out what was happening. Taylor had taken Mom out to a Sugar Chair.

Taylor must be reminding Mom of what Grandma would want them to do:

Slow Down,
Look Around,
Figure Out How to Sweeten Things Up

They were outside talking for a long time. And when Taylor and Mom came back in, Buddy could hear Mom say, "Thanks, Taylor. I needed that. I'm just going to love her through it, no matter what. It doesn't matter if she remembers me. It just matters that I love her the best way I can. That's what she needs."

Taylor hugged her again and said, "that sounds like a good plan, Mom."

Buddy thought so too.

About the Authors:

<u>Dr. Mark David Milliron</u> is an award-winning leader, author, speaker, and consultant who works with universities, community colleges, K-12 schools, foundations, corporations, associations, and government agencies across the country and around the world. He serves as Senior Vice President and Executive Dean of the Teachers College at Western Governors University (WGU). In addition to his work with WGU, Mark helps catalyze positive change in education through his Catalytic Conversations blog and podcast series, and also through service on the boards and advisory councils of leading-edge education organizations, including the Trellis Foundation; Bennett College; the Global Online Academy; Civitas Learning; the Mastery Transcript Consortium; the Hope Center for College, Community, & Justice; and ISKME/Open Education Resource Commons. He also holds an appointment as a Professor of Practice in the College of Education at The University of Texas at Austin..

Regardless of all his activities and accomplishments, he will quickly tell you that the most important job and the greatest blessing in his life is serving as Julia's husband, and as father to Alexandra, Richard, Marcus, and Max.

You can learn more about Mark's work at <u>www.markmilliron.com</u>

 Alexandra "Alex" Joy Milliron is a rising senior in the College of Education at the University of Texas at Austin. During her time at Dripping Springs High School (TX), she was an honor student, a three-year varsity basketball player and high jumper, and regular community volunteer. In addition, she helped coach youth basketball, working with grades 2nd through 6th. During her time at UT Austin, she has served as a children's Tae Kwan Do instructor, nanny, and as an officer of the Texas Darlins—the spirit club supporting University of Texas at Austin Basketball. Currently, she is preparing for graduate school and a career as a teacher, coach, and community leader – and power Mom to her puppy "Bento."

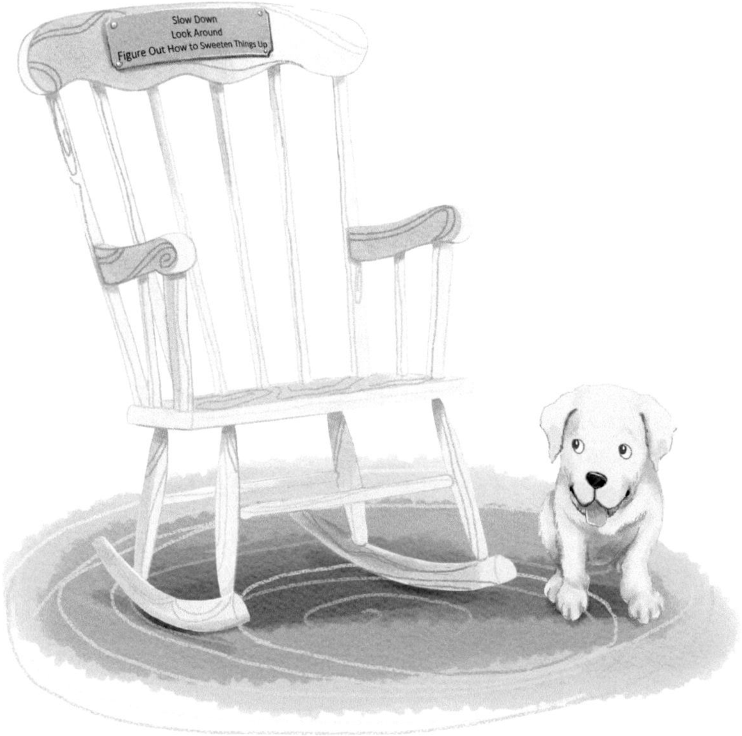
Slow Down
Look Around
Figure Out How to Sweeten Things Up

Printed in the United States
By Bookmasters